stories for Girls

tiger tales

Contents

A Little Fairy Magic

by Julia Hubery   Illustrated by Alison Edgson

It was Abby's birthday, and she was bubbling with excitement in her new fairy costume. She loved her shimmery wings and her floaty pink dress.

"Look at my wings! Look at my starry wand!" she squeaked, twirling and whirling.

"Now I'm a real, real fairy!" she sang, as she spun and danced.

"You're a fairy princess," smiled Daddy, "and you need an enchanted castle. Come and look . . . ."

Abby peeked into her bedroom.

"Wow!" she whispered.
Her bedroom sparkled with more
birthday presents—new stars and
twinkles and silvery sprinkles.

"Make us some magic, Abby," said
her big brother Sam.

"I'm going to fly first!" said Abby.

She raced into the garden and scrambled up onto the old tree stump.

I will fly just like a fairy, she thought.

She stood on tiptoe and stretched her arms.

She jumped high into the air,
waving her wand . . .

. . . and landed BUMP!
in the flower bed.

"Oh, dear," sighed Abby. "Maybe flying is too hard for a brand-new fairy. I'll practice making wishes instead."

She decided to start with a wish for Sam.

He was playing pirates in the kiddie pool.
"I'm Fairy Flowerbelle," Abby announced.
"Tell me your wish, and I'll make it come true!"
"Go away, pesky pixie, or you'll walk the
plank!" Sam growled.

"I'm not a pixie!" Abby stamped. "Now make a wish, or I'll turn you into a frog!"

"All right," Sam laughed. "I wish I had a parrot."

Abby skipped happily through the garden. "What shall I use for a parrot?" she wondered . . . .

. . . and there, on a leaf, she spotted a ladybug.

Perfect, she thought, and began her spell.

"Ibb-bib-bob –
oh, stay still!

"Tip-tap-top –
stop flying!

"Oh, you silly ladybug,
come back!" she shouted
as it zoomed away.

"I'm not a very good fairy,"
Abby sighed to Mommy
and Daddy. "I can't fly, and I
can't make a parrot by magic."

"That's OK," said Daddy.
"We need some magic here.
You can add fairy sprinkles
to the cupcakes for your
birthday party—yummy!"

Abby made the cakes look so special,
she felt just like a fairy again.
"I'm going to tell Sam I really
can do magic!" she said.

But poor Sam was upset.
The mast of his ship had
snapped in two.
"It's broken," he said sadly.
"Now I can't be a pirate anymore."

"Don't worry! I'll fix it!" said Abby.
"My magic's getting better. I just
needed practice!"

Abby twirled twice, then tapped the mast gently. Nothing happened.

She thought and thought. "I know," she said. "We'll close our eyes and wish very hard."

Sam closed his eyes, but Abby tiptoed to the boat. "One . . . two . . . three . . . fiddle-de-dee . . ." she whispered.

"Ta-daaa!"

Sam opened his eyes . . . and saw a sparkling new mast on his pirate ship.

"You really can do magic, Fairy Flowerbelle!" he laughed.

"I did, I did!" squealed Abby, and they sailed together until Daddy called, "Ahoy there! It's party-time!"

Mommy and Daddy, Abby
and Sam shared a wonderful
fairy birthday feast.

"I like being a fairy," yawned
Abby as the stars began to shine.
"You are a fantastic fairy," said
Mommy, "but even birthday
fairies need their sleep."
And she carried Abby
up to her fairy castle.

As Mommy kissed her good-night, Abby whispered in her ear, "I didn't really do fairy magic, Mommy."

"Oh, yes, you did," said Mommy. "You were kind and thoughtful, and you helped Sam feel happy. That's the best fairy magic in the world."

Princess Dolly
and the
SECRET
LOCKET

by Alice Wood

Dolly was in her little attic room at the
top of the Big House, when she heard
the buzz of excited voices coming
in through the window.

"What's going on down there?"
she asked her dear friend Birdie.
"Come on! Let's find out."

Quickly, Dolly cleaned up her sewing and put on her special locket, then rushed out along the street.

There was a crowd of people gathered around a big poster. Her friends Sally and Sue were already there, and Cook was reading aloud . . .

The **Duke & Duchess**
(HOME AT LAST FROM
THEIR WILD TRAVELS)

ANNOUNCE A

Grand Ball
for the
Royal Princess

SATURDAY AT 6 O'CLOCK
THE BALLROOM ~ THE BIG HOUSE

Everyone is invited!

"Well, imagine that!" gasped Cook.
"There's so much to do! Come on, everyone!"
"A real princess, coming here!" said Dolly.
"I wonder what she'll be like."

"Do you think she's very graceful?" asked Sue.
    "Oh, yes!" said Dolly.

"I bet she never gets her hands dirty!" Harry decided.

"She must have a lot of servants," said Cook. *That would be nice,* Dolly thought.

"I expect she has baths full of rose-petal perfume and sweet lavender," said Rufus.

"How wonderful," Dolly sighed.

Dolly, Sally, and Sue scrubbed and polished, dusted and cleaned until the whole house shone. Then they all flopped down at the kitchen table.

"What are you girls wearing to the Ball?" asked Cook, looking at their dirty clothes. "You want to look your best for the princess, don't you?"

"Ooooh, yes!" they agreed.

Dolly got her sewing basket and they
chose some pretty material – purple
for Sally and yellow for Sue.

Dolly helped them with the tricky parts and by
dinnertime, Sally and Sue were clutching their
beautiful new dresses and waving good bye.

But then there was a tap-tap-tapping on the attic door. Three little toys were standing outside, looking up at Dolly with big, round eyes.

"We need your help!" squeaked Teddy.

"Come on in," Dolly smiled.

She stitched a flowery
patch onto Teddy's
pants . . .

some pink satin ribbons
onto Lily's ballet slippers . . .

. . . and some pretty flowers
around Bunny's hat.

"You are the kindest Dolly
ever!" they giggled, heading
back home to bed.

Dolly worked late into the evening
finishing her own special dress. That night
she dreamed of dancing under the
shimmering moon while Birdie
flew around the bright stars, singing.

Early next morning, there was another knock at the door. This time it was Sue.

"Oh, Dolly!" she cried. "I tried on my dress and spilled my juice and now it's ruined and I don't have anything else to wear!"

In a heartbeat, Dolly decided to give her own special dress to Sue. "Look, I made a spare one, just in case. You can wear it if you'd like."

Sue blinked away her tears. "You're the best friend *ever!*" she sniffed, and gave Dolly an enormous hug.

"Oh, Birdie!" Dolly sighed.
"What am I going to wear now?"

Suddenly, Birdie soared up into the air.
He dropped something golden and glittering into her lap.

"My locket!" Dolly smiled.
"My beautiful golden locket!
I can still look my best
without a new dress.
I am a lucky Dolly."

At last it was the evening of the Grand Ball. As the Duke and Duchess stepped out of their splendid coach, everyone gathered around excitedly.

"Greetings to you all on this wonderful evening," said the Duchess. "We are so looking forward to meeting your princess. Is she here?"

Confused whispers rippled through the crowd. "What does she mean?"

"There isn't a princess here!" Harry called out.
"We thought she was coming with you!"

"Well, this is *very* awkward," said the Duke.
"The princess must be here. She was brought
to the Big House as a baby, years ago.
She would be a little girl by now . . . ."

"Really? And we never knew? Whatever could have happened?" asked Cook. "How will we find her now?"

"She might still have her royal locket," replied the Duchess, "just like mine. Look . . . ."

"We know someone with a locket exactly like that one!" called Sally and Sue . . .

"Princess Dolly!"

"Oh my goodness!" Dolly gasped.
"Me? A princess?"

"Dear Princess Dolly," the Duchess smiled
warmly, "this royal trunk belongs to you."
Inside was the most beautiful ballgown
Dolly had ever seen.

Sally and Sue helped her try on her
precious new things. "We're so glad
it's you!" they whispered.

Everybody was delighted. They could not have wished for a kinder princess than the lovely Princess Dolly!

The Tiniest Mermaid

by Laura Garnham

Illustrated by

Patricia MacCarthy

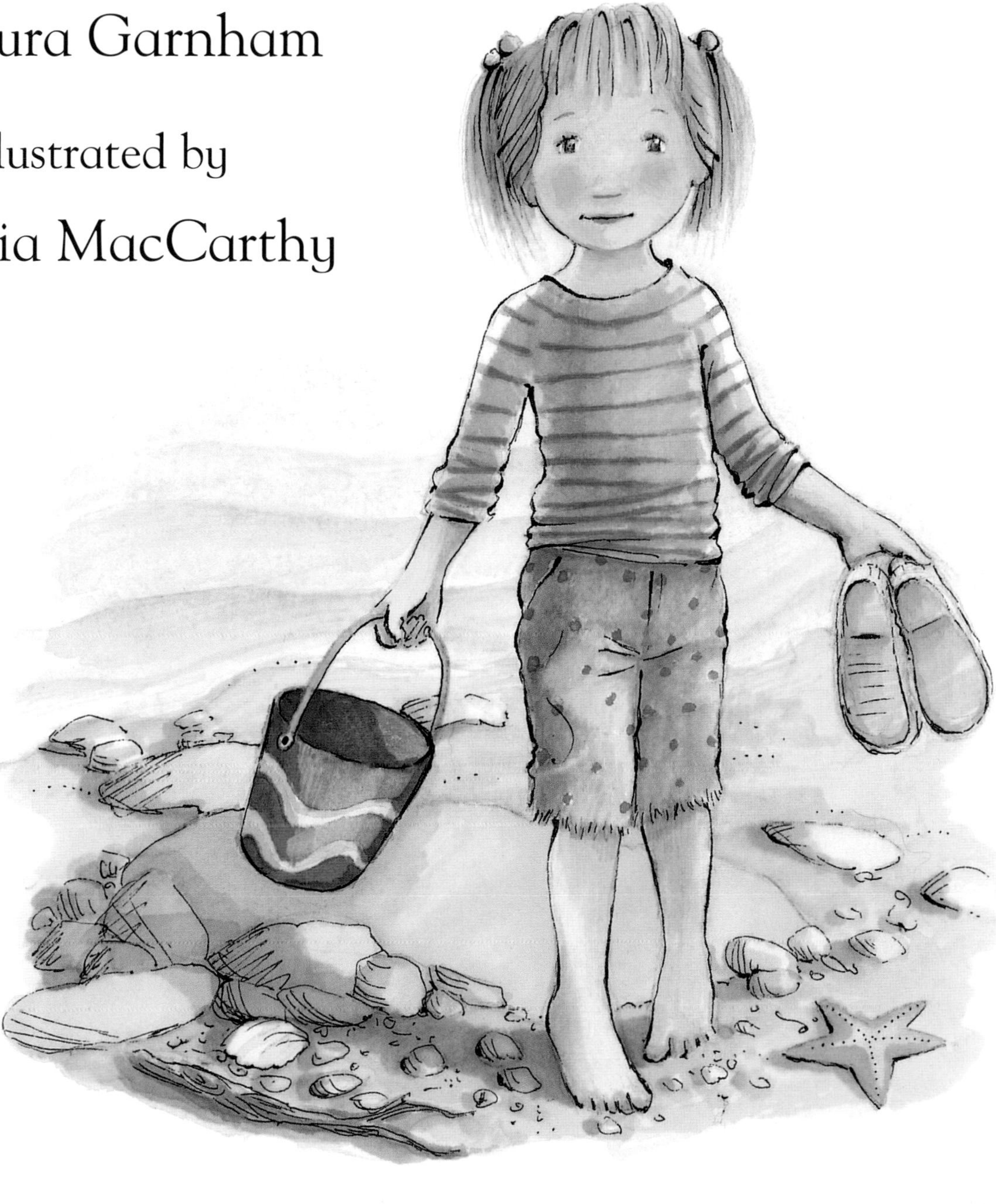

Lily lived by the wide blue sea.
On summer nights she would sit on
the beach, gazing out over the waves,
dreaming of magic and adventure.

One night, as she sat by the rock pools,
a faint sparkle caught her eye and a little
voice cried out, "Help! Please help me!"

Lily gasped. It was a mermaid! A beautiful, tiny mermaid! Was she dreaming? But the mermaid called out again, "Help me, please! My tail was hurt in the storm last night, and I can't get back home!"

"Oh, you poor thing!" said Lily, kneeling
by the rock pool. "I'll help you, if I can."
"Thank you," whispered the mermaid.
"You'll be safe with me," said Lily softly.
"I'll take care of you."

Lily scooped the delicate mermaid from the water. She walked carefully up the steps, through the house to her room.

By her bed was a huge glass fish tank, the perfect place for a mermaid to rest.

As she slipped into the water the tiny mermaid smiled. "I'm Jewel. What's your name?"

"Lily," said Lily, smiling back at her new friend.

That night, Lily sat up for a long time, watching over Jewel as she slept. "I just knew mermaids were real!" Lily said. Then she whispered to the fish, "Now let her sleep and get better."

The next morning, Lily leaped out of bed and rushed to the fish tank. Had it all been a dream? She stared anxiously through the glass and there, in the castle, was Jewel!

"You're still here!" Lily cried with delight.

"Of course," laughed Jewel. "Where would I be?"

Jewel was looking much better, and Lily saw that her tail was twinkling gently. She thought she had never seen anything so beautiful in all her life.

Lily and Jewel talked all day. Jewel spoke of a world where mermaids swam through the coral, playing with sea horses. Lily could almost feel the water and see the light and color of the ocean.

That night, her dreams were filled with magic and mermaids and a special place far, far under the sea.

Slowly Jewel grew stronger. As her magic returned, her tail sparkled brighter, and she transformed the tank into a shimmering underwater wonderland.

Lily raced home after school each day, and she and Jewel talked and talked until they were the best of friends.

"I wish I were a mermaid," said Lily one night.
"It is wonderful," Jewel said wistfully. "My friends and I travel the entire world helping trapped or hurt animals. And sometimes we use our sparkling tails to guide sailors home through terrible storms."

"Wow!" said Lily in wonder. "I never knew!"

"It's exciting, but it can be very scary," said Jewel. "When I was hurt in that awful storm, I was separated from my friends by a huge wave and thrown onto the rocks." She sighed. "They must be wondering what happened to me."

Lily gasped. Jewel's friends would be worried about her.

"Oh, Jewel," she cried. "You must go back to your friends!"

"Yes, I must," said Jewel. "But I will miss you."

"If only we didn't have to say good-bye!" sighed Lily. "I wish I could come with you. Or just visit your magical world."

Jewel smiled suddenly. "I could show you, if you'd like. Close your eyes . . . ."

Lily took a deep breath as Jewel started singing a gentle song. Lily could feel magic all around her and hear the rush of the ocean growing louder . . . .

All at once, she was there with Jewel, swimming with dolphins as they danced and dived through the water. Further and further they swam through the warm blue ocean until the setting sun turned the white beaches gold.

When Lily fell asleep that night,
she could still hear the dolphin's song
and feel the sand between her toes.

The next morning, Lily cradled Jewel in her
hands for the very last time as she carried her to
the seashore.

"Don't be sad, Lily," said Jewel softly, and
she gave her a special shell. "Whenever you miss
me, put the shell to your ear and you will hear
the magic of the sea whispering inside."

With a flick of her glittering tail, the tiny mermaid swam off. But as she waved good-bye, Lily saw two more shining tails appear at Jewel's side. Jewel was with her friends, and she was safe. And Lily knew that whenever she missed her, she could listen to the sounds of the shell and look for the sparkles glimmering in the sea, for Jewel would always be near.

The Wish Cat

by Ragnhild Scamell

Illustrated by Gaby Hansen

Holly's house had a cat flap. It was
a small door in the big door so a cat
could come and go.

But Holly didn't have a cat.

One night, something magical
happened. Holly saw a falling star.

As the star trailed across the sky, she
made a wish.

"I wish I had a kitten," she whispered.
"A tiny cuddly kitten who could jump in
and out of the cat flap."

CRASH!

Something big landed on the windowsill outside. It wasn't a kitten . . . .

It was Tom, the scruffiest, most raggedy cat Holly had ever seen. He sat there in the moonlight, smiling a crooked smile.

"Meo-o-ow!"

"I'm Tom, your wish cat," he seemed to say.

"It's a mistake," cried Holly.
"I wished for a kitten."
Tom didn't think Holly
had made a mistake.

He rubbed his torn ear
against the window and
howled so loudly it made
him cough and splutter.

"Meo-o-ow, o-o-w, o-o-w!"

Holly hid under her
comforter, hoping that
he'd go away.

The next morning, Tom was still there, waiting for her outside the cat flap. He wanted to come in, and he had brought her a present of a smelly old piece of fish.

"Yuck!" said Holly. She picked it up and dropped it in the garbage can. Tom looked puzzled. "Bad cat," she said, shooing him away.

"Go on, go home!" cried Holly, walking to her swing.

But Tom got there
before she did. He
sharpened his claws
on the swing . . .

and washed his coat
noisily, pulling out
bits of fur and spitting
them everywhere.

At lunchtime, Tom sat on the
windowsill, watching Holly eat.

She broke off a piece of her sandwich and
passed it out to him through the cat flap.
Tom gobbled it down, purring all the while.

In the afternoon, a cold wind swept through the garden, and Holly had to wear her jacket and scarf. Tom didn't seem to feel the cold. He followed her around . . .

chasing leaves . . .

balancing along the
top of the fence . . .

showing off.

Soon it was time for
Holly to go inside.
"Bye, Tom," she said,
and stroked his head.

Tom followed her to the door and
settled himself by the cat flap.

That evening, it snowed. Gleaming pompoms of snow danced in the air.

Outside the cat flap, Tom curled himself into a ragged ball to keep warm. Soon there was a white cushion of snow all over the doorstep, and on Tom.

Holly heard him meowing miserably. She ran to the cat flap and held it open . . . .

Tom came in, shaking snow
all over the kitchen floor.
"Poor old Tom," said Holly.

He ate a large plate of food, and drank
an even larger bowl of warm milk.
Tom purred louder than ever when
Holly dried him with the kitchen towel.

Soon Tom had settled
down, snug on Holly's bed.
Holly stroked his scruffy fur,
and together they watched
the glittering stars.

Then, suddenly, another
star fell. Holly couldn't think
of a single thing to wish
for. She had everything she
wanted. And so did Tom.

Fairy Friends

by Claire Freedman

Illustrated by Gail Yerrill

Among the garden flowers,
In the leafy, dappled light,
The tiny friendship fairies live,
Hiding out of sight!

In their shimmery, secret world,
They love to be together.
Their lives are extra-magical
As friendship lasts for ever!

Wishing on a dewdrop,
Sparkling in the sun.
Sharing dreams of happiness
And magic fairy fun!

Catch a glimpse of glistening wing?
Feel a tingle on your skin?

Fluttering fairies are close by,
Sprinkling gold dust as they fly,

Making every dream come true,
Wishing happiness for you!

There's a beautiful petal trail
That leads to a magical place,
Where the scent of rosebuds fills the air
In a patchwork of soft pink lace.

Here the fairies rest their wings
As dragonflies hover above,
For good times are even more special
When shared with the friends they love.

Puff of stardust on their wings,
Now the fairy fun begins!

Jumping over toadstools,
Dancing with the bees,
Playing catch with ladybugs
In grass as tall as trees.

Swinging on a spider's web,
Skipping with a friend,
Finding golden fairy dust
At the rainbow's end!

Everyone's happy; it's party time!
The fairies have so much to do –
Ballgowns to sew, made from petals,
And ivy-leaf bags to make, too!

The fairies all help with the baking,
Piping cream onto tiny iced tarts.
There are strawberry buns and fun fairy fizz,
And sandwiches cut into hearts!

As dusk falls, the lanterns are twinkling;
The garden's aglow in the light.
So, to the soft chime of the music,
Off they fly for a magical night!

Picking flower petals,
Gathering the dew,
Flying with the baby birds,
Painting rainbows, too!

Looking out for others,
Helping someone new,
Making friends with everyone—
That's what fairies do!

Sharing a daisy umbrella,
We hop in a tree hole and hide.
Who cares if it's raining and chilly?
Together we feel warm inside.

When the weather's dull and gray,
Or too wet outdoors to play,
Fairy friends have lots of fun
In their fairy style salon.

Sharing secret fashion tips,
While outside the rain drip-drips.
For like rainbows after rain,
Friends make you feel bright again!

Best friends know this to be true:
Everything's more fun with two.
Happy chatting, hour by hour,
Curled up cozy, in a flower.

Swapping secrets, holding hands,
Knowing your friend understands,
Sharing wishes from the heart,
Certain that you'll never part.
Talking about anything—
This is what best friendships bring!

At the bottom of the tree stump,
Where the garden almost ends,
There's a spot where all the fairies
Leave out treasures for their friends.

Fairy gifts are made with care,
Like trinkets formed of flowers,
Wrapped in petals, moss, or leaves,
From magic fairy bowers.

Each tiny token means a lot,
A small keepsake to treasure.
For like their special fairy gifts,
True friendship lasts forever.

When stars glitter in the sky
And the moon gleams up on high,
Under shady ferns we lie,
While the breeze blows like a sigh.
Much too sleepy now to play,
Sharing stories ends our day.

Stars light the sky,
Fireflies flash by,
The garden glows silver and bright.
Shadows soon creep,
Time now to sleep—
Sweet dreams, gentle fairies,
good night!

Meet the Fairy Friends!

Being a friend to everyone,
Making your dreams come true,
Always there to show they care—
That's what fairy friends do!

DEWDROP

Dewdrop
is bubbly, talkative,
and loves to giggle.

POPPY

Poppy
is kind, trustworthy,
and always sticks up
for her friends.

RAINBOW

Rainbow
is creative, imaginative,
and always has
great ideas.

The Princess's Secret Sleepover

by Hilary Robinson   Illustrated by Mandy Stanley

I just got back from a sleepover party at my friend Amy's house. Her address is 2 Palace Place. It made me wonder what it's like to sleep in a real palace. I'm going to write to my friend Princess Isabella and ask her.

38 Sunny Lane,
Townsville

Dear Princess Isabella
I was wondering what it's
like sleeping in a palace. Do you
have a canopy bed with
curtains on it and are your
nightgowns made from silk?

Love Lucy
x x x x x

Dear Lucy,

   Princess Isabella has asked me to write and thank you for your letter.

   The Princess's bed does have satin curtains, and she has a lot of silk nightgowns.

But secretly, she prefers to wear . . .

. . . spotted pajamas!

38 Sunny Lane,
Townsville

Dear Princess Isabella
Thank you for your letter.
My favorite toy dog, Snuggles,
always comes with me to
sleepovers and sits on my
pillow while I sleep. Can you tell
me do princesses have special
toys to watch over them
at night?

Love Lucy

Dear Lucy,

Princess Isabella has asked me to thank you for your letter and to say that she is given many beautiful dolls that sit in glass cabinets in her bedroom.

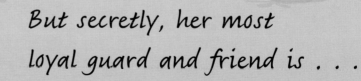

But secretly, her most
loyal guard and friend is . . .

. . . Trusty!

154

38 Sunny Lane,
Townsville

Dear Princess Isabella

Are princesses allowed to stay up late at sleepovers? Amy and I make up songs because we want to be famous one day. We use our hairbrushes for microphones.

Love Lucy
x x x

Dear Lucy,

Princess Isabella has asked me to write to say that she is allowed to stay up late listening to the royal storyteller.

But secretly, when he's gone
to bed, the royal maids sneak in . . .

. . . *to sing in their girl band,*
Isabella and the Dusty Daisies!

38 Sunny Lane,
Townsville

Dear Princess Isabella
Your girl band sounds great.
Amy and I love making friendship
bracelets and braiding each
other's hair before we go to bed.
Do you ever do that?
× Love Lucy × × ×
× ×
P.S. I'm sending you a
friendship bracelet.

159

Dear Lucy,

Princess Isabella has asked me to write and say thank you for the lovely friendship bracelet. When her cousin Princess Sophia comes to visit, their hair is brushed one hundred times with a silver hairbrush.

But secretly, when no one else
is around, they like to do . . .

161

. . . face painting!

Last night, I had a great idea for something else we could do at a sleepover. I was so excited that I had to write to Princess Isabella to tell her all about it.

38 Sunny Lane,
Townsville

Dear Princess Isabella
At our next sleepover Amy and I
are going to have cookies in the
shape of crowns and goblets
of milk. Can you tell me if
princesses are served big banquets
at sleepovers?

+ Love Lucy + + +

yummy!

milk

Dear Lucy,

The Princess has asked me to write to say that while many royal princesses do eat banquets at sleepovers, the Princess and her loyal friend Trusty prefer midnight feasts. They would be delighted if, on the Princess's birthday this year, you might be kind enough to . . .

. . . *join them!*

STORIES FOR GIRLS

tiger tales
5 River Road, Suite 128, Wilton, CT 06897
Published in the United States 2015
Originally published in Great Britain 2015 by Little Tiger Press
This volume copyright © 2015 Little Tiger Press
Cover artwork copyright © 2011 Alison Edgson, 2001 Gaby Hansen,
2007 Gail Yerril, 2010, 2011 Rachel Baines
Additional artwork © 2010, 2011 Rachel Baines
ISBN-13: 978-1-58925-536-4
ISBN-10: 1-58925-536-4
Printed in China • LTP/1800/0981/0914

For more insight and activities,
visit us at www.tigertalesbooks.com

THE WISH CAT

by Ragnhild Scamell
Illustrated by Gaby Hansen

First published in Great Britain 2001
by Little Tiger Press

Text copyright © 2001 Ragnhild Scamell
Illustrations copyright © 2001 Gaby Hansen

FAIRY FRIENDS

by Claire Freedman
Illustrated by Gail Yerrill

First published in Great Britain 2007
by Little Tiger Press

Text copyright © 2007, 2014 Claire Freedman
Illustrations copyright © 2007, 2014 Gail Yerrill

THE PRINCESS'S SECRET SLEEPOVER

by Hilary Robinson
Illustrated by Mandy Stanley

First published in Great Britain 2007
by Little Tiger Press

Text copyright © 2007 Hilary Robinson
Illustrations copyright © 2007 Mandy Stanley